ALL
CREATURES
GREAT
AND SMALL

ALL CREATURES GREAT AND SMALL

ILLUMINATED BY
ISABELLE BRENT

Little, Brown and Company
Boston Toronto London

FOR CLAIRE
AND HER SON ROBERT PAUL FISHER

First Edition

Published in Great Britain by Pavilion Books Limited

"Furry Bear" from *Now We Are Six* by A. A. Milne. Copyright 1927
by E. P. Dutton, renewed © 1955 by A. A. Milne. Used by
permission of Dutton Children's Books, a division of Penguin Books
USA. "The Yak" by Hilaire Belloc, reprinted by permission of the
Peters Fraser & Dunlop Group Ltd. "Diary of a Church Mouse" by
John Betjeman, reprinted by permission of John Murray
(Publishers) Ltd.

ISBN 0-316-10869-3

Library of Congress Catalog Card Number 93-86153

10 9 8 7 6 5 4 3 2 1

Printed in Hong Kong

Produced by Mandarin Offset

CONTENTS

TWO LITTLE KITTENS

ANONYMOUS

Two little kittens, one stormy night,
Began to quarrel, and then to fight;
One had a mouse, the other had none,
And that's the way the quarrel begun.

'I'll have that mouse,' said the biggest cat;
'You'll have that mouse? We'll see about that!'
'I *will* have that mouse,' said the eldest son;
'You *shan't* have that mouse,' said the little one.

I told you before 'twas a stormy night
When these two kittens began to fight;
The old woman seized her sweeping broom,
And swept the two kittens right out of the room.

The ground was covered with frost and snow,
And the two little kittens had nowhere to go;
So they laid them down on the mat at the door,
While the old woman finished sweeping the floor.

Then they crept in, as quiet as mice,
All wet with the snow, and as cold as ice,
For they found it was better, that stormy night,
To lie down and sleep than to quarrel and fight.

HABITS OF THE HIPPOPOTAMUS

BY ARTHUR GUITERMAN

The hippopotamus is strong
And huge of head and broad of bustle;
The limbs on which he rolls along
Are big with hippopotamuscle.

He does not greatly care for sweets
Like ice cream, apple pie or custard,
But takes to flavor what he eats
A little hippopotomustard.

The hippopotamus is true
To all his principles, and just;
He always tries his best to do
The things one hippopotamust.

He never rides in trucks and trams,
In taxicabs or omnibuses,
And so keeps out of traffic jams
And other hippopotamusses.

DIARY OF A CHURCH MOUSE

BY SIR JOHN BETJEMAN

Here among long-discarded cassocks,
Damp stools, and half-split open hassocks,
Here where the Vicar never looks
I nibble through old service books,
Lean and alone I spend my days
Behind this Church of England baize.
I share my dark forgotten room
With two oil-lamps and half a broom.
The cleaner never bothers me,
So here I eat my frugal tea.
My bread is sawdust mixed with straw;
My jam is polish for the floor.

　　Christmas and Easter may be feasts
For congregations and for priests,
And so may Whitsun. All the same,
They do not fill my meagre frame.
For me the only feast at all
Is Autumn's Harvest Festival,
When I can satisfy my want
With ears of corn around the font.
I climb the eagle's brazen head
To burrow through a loaf of bread.
I scramble up the pulpit stair
And gnaw the marrows hanging there.

　　It is enjoyable to taste
These items ere they go to waste,
But how annoying when one finds
That other mice with pagan minds
Come into church my food to share
Who have no proper business there.
Two field mice who have no desire

To be baptized, invade the choir.
A large and most unfriendly rat
Comes in to see what we are at.
He says he thinks there is no God
And yet he comes . . . it's rather odd.
This year he stole a sheaf of wheat
(It screened our special preacher's seat),
And prosperous mice from fields away
Come in to hear the organ play,
And under cover of its notes
Ate through the altar's sheaf of oats.
A Low Church mouse, who thinks that I
Am too papistical, and High,
Yet somehow doesn't think it wrong
To munch through Harvest Evensong,
While I, who starve the whole year through,
Must share my food with rodents who
Except at this time of the year
Not once inside the church appear.

　　Within the human world I know
Such goings-on could not be so,
For human beings only do
What their religion tells them to.
They read the Bible every day
And always, night and morning, pray,
And just like me, the good church mouse,
Worship each week in God's own house.

　　But all the same it's strange to me
How very full the church can be
With people I don't see at all
Except at Harvest Festival.

THE YAK

BY HILAIRE BELLOC

As a friend to the children, commend me the yak,
You will find it exactly the thing:
It will carry and fetch, you can ride on its back,
Or lead it about with a string.

The Tartar who dwells in the plains of Tibet
(A desolate region of snow),
Has for centuries made it a nursery pet,
And surely the Tartar should know!

Then tell your papa where the yak can be got,
And if he is awfully rich,
He will buy you the creature — or else he will not:
I cannot be positive which.

THE OWL AND THE PUSSY-CAT

BY EDWARD LEAR

The Owl and the Pussy-Cat went to sea
In a beautiful pea-green boat;
They took some honey and plenty of
    money,
Wrapped up in a five-pound note.
The Owl looked up to the stars above,
And sang to a small guitar,
'O lovely Pussy! O Pussy, my love,
What a beautiful Pussy you are,
             You are,
             You are!
What a beautiful Pussy you are!'

Pussy said to the Owl, 'You elegant fowl!
How charmingly sweet you sing!
O let us be married! too long we have
    tarried:
But what shall we do for a ring?'
They sailed away for a year and a day,
To the land where the Bong-tree grows,
And there in a wood a Piggy-wig stood,
With a ring at the end of his nose.
             His nose
             His nose,
With a ring at the end of his nose.

'Dear Pig, are you willing to sell for one shilling
Your ring?' Said the Piggy, 'I will.'
So they took it away and were married next day
By the Turkey who lives on the hill.
They dined on mince and slices of quince
Which they ate with a runcible spoon;
And hand in hand, on the edge of the sand,
They danced by the light of the moon,
             The moon
             The moon,
They danced by the light of the moon.

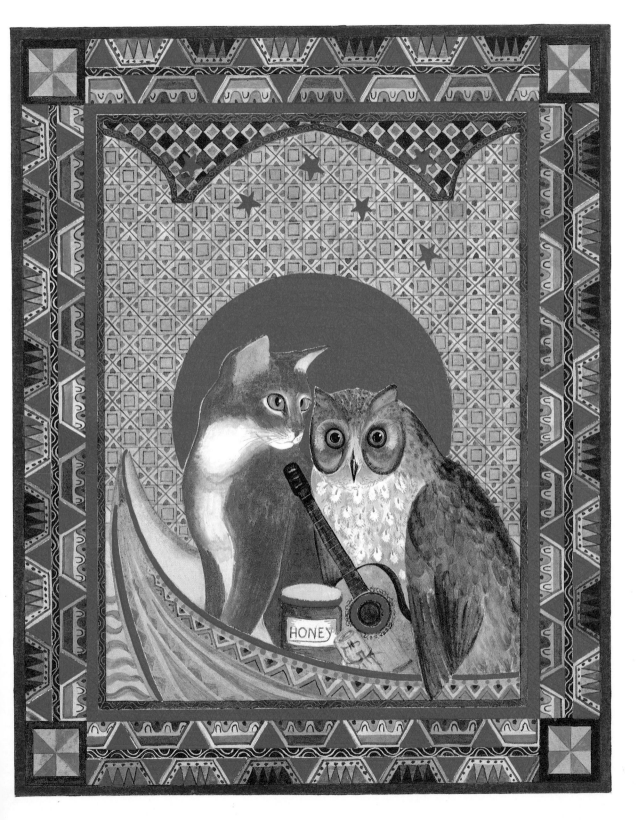

THE BLIND MEN AND THE ELEPHANT

BY JOHN GODFREY-SAXE

It was six men of Indostan
To learning much inclined,
Who went to see the Elephant
(Though all of them were blind),
That each by observation
Might satisfy his mind.

The first approached the Elephant,
And happening to fall
Against his broad and sturdy side,
At once began to bawl:
'God bless me! But the Elephant,
Is very like a wall!'

The second, feeling of the tusk,
Cried, 'Ho! what have we here
So very round and smooth and sharp?
To me 'tis mighty clear
This wonder of an Elephant
Is very like a spear!'

The third approached the animal,
And happening to take
The squirming trunk within his hands,
Thus boldly up and spake:
'I see,' quoth he, 'the Elephant
Is very like a snake!'

The fourth reached out an eager hand,
And felt about the knee.
'What most this wondrous beast is like
Is mighty plain,' quoth he;
'Tis clear enough the Elephant
Is very like a tree!'

The fifth who chanced to touch the ear,
Said: 'E'en the blindest man
Can tell what this resembles most;
Deny the fact who can,
This marvel of an Elephant
Is very like a fan!'

The sixth no sooner had begun
About the beast to grope,
Than, seizing on the swinging tail
That fell within his scope,
'I see' quoth he, 'the Elephant
Is very like a rope!'

And so these men of Indostan
Disputed loud and long,
Each in his own opinion
Exceeding stiff and strong,
Though each was partly in the right,
And all were in the wrong!

So oft in theologic wars,
The disputants, I ween,
Rail on in utter ignorance
Of what each other mean,
And prate about an Elephant
Not one of them has seen!

THE CAMEL'S LAMENT

BY CHARLES CARRYL

Canary-birds feed on sugar and seed,
Parrots have crackers to crunch;
And as for the poodles, they tell me the
    noodles
Have chickens and cream for their lunch.
But there's never a question
About MY digestion —
Anything does for me!

Cats, you're aware, can repose in
    a chair,
Chickens can roost upon rails;
Puppies are able to sleep in a stable,
And oysters can slumber in pails.
But no one supposes
A poor Camel dozes —
Any place does for me!

Lambs are enclosed where it's never exposed.
Coops are constructed for hens;
Kittens are treated to houses well heated,
And pigs are protected by pens.
But a Camel comes handy
Wherever it's sandy —
Anywhere does for me!

People would laugh if you rode a giraffe,
Or mounted the back of an ox;
It's nobody's habit to ride on a rabbit,
Or try to bestraddle a fox.
But as for a Camel, he's
Ridden by families —
Any load does for me!

A snake is as round as a hole in the ground,
And weasels are wavy and sleek;
And no alligator could ever be straighter
Than lizards that live in a creek.
But a Camel's all lumpy
And bumpy and humpy —
ANY shape does for me!

Furry Bear

BY A. A. MILNE

If I were a bear,
And a big bear too,
I shouldn't much care
If it froze or snew
I shouldn't much mind
If it snowed or friz
I'd be all fur-lined
With a coat like this!

For I'd have fur boots and a brown fur wrap,
And brown fur knickers and a big fur cap
I'd have a fur muffle-ruff to cover my jaws
And brown fur mittens on my big brown paws.
With a big brown furry-down up to my head,
I'd sleep all the winter in a big fur bed.

THE BUTTERFLY'S BALL

BY WILLIAM ROSCOE

Come take up your hats, and away let us haste,
To the Butterfly's Ball, and the Grasshopper's Feast.
The trumpeter Gadfly has summoned the crew,
And the revels are now only waiting for you.

On the smooth-shaven grass by the side of a wood,
Beneath a broad oak which for ages has stood,
See the children of earth and the tenants of air,
For an evening's amusement together repair.

And there came the Beetle, so blind and so black,
Who carried the Emmet, his friend, on his back.
And there came the Gnat, and the Dragonfly too,
And all their relations, green, orange, and blue.

And there came the Moth, with her plumage of down,
And the Hornet, with jacket of yellow and brown;
Who with him the Wasp, his companion did bring,
But they promised that evening, to lay by their sting.

Then the sly little Dormouse crept out of his hole,
And led to the feast his blind cousin the Mole.
And the Snail, with his horns peeping out of his shell,
Came, fatigued with the distance, the length of an ell.

A mushroom their table, and on it was laid
A water-dock leaf, which a tablecloth made.
The viands were various, to each of their taste,
And the Bee brought the honey to sweeten the feast.

With steps most majestic the Snail did advance,
And he promised the gazers a minuet to dance:
But they all laughed so loud that he drew in his head,
And went in his own little chamber to bed.

Then, as evening gave way to the shadows of night,
Their watchman, the Glow-worm, came out with his light.
So home let us hasten, while yet we can see;
For no watchman is waiting for you and for me.

THE CROCODILE

BY LEWIS CARROLL

How doth the little crocodile
Improve his shining tail,
And pour the waters of the Nile
On every golden scale!

How cheerfully he seems to grin,
How neatly spreads his claws,
And welcomes little fishes in,
With gently smiling jaws!